D1208967

2/22/2023

Whatever the
future holds, I hope
good FORTUNE will always
smile upon you.

Warmest regards -
Maritta
×
Haifa

# HOPE
## and
# FORTUNE

Written by
## Marissa Bañez

Illustrated by
Enroc Illustrations
In Collaboration With
Marissa Bañez

One day, a young girl played with a beautiful butterfly.

Feeling happy, she chased it into the Fabled Fairy Forest,
but it quickly flew far away, leaving her alone.

Her name was Esperanza, which means "hope" but right now Esperanza had hopelessly lost her way.

She was very sad and very scared.


Golden Tree
wanted to help Esperanza and so he said:


Deep into the Fabled Fairy Forest you should go

To learn everything you need to know.

Sometimes we all need someone for guidance.

It's scary but we don't need to suffer in silence.

So find the twelve Fortune Fairies at all cost.

They will help you to never again feel lost.

When she saw the first Fortune Fairy,
Esperanza said:


Fortune Fairy, if you don't mind,
I'm really in quite a bind.
I really need your help right now.
I don't know what to do or how.
I've lost my way, can't seem to get back.
Golden Tree said you'd get me on the right track.

The fairy said:

I'm the Fortune Fairy of Hope.

All the Fortune Fairies will help you cope.

Give yourself permission to cry.

Just know that things will get better as time goes by.

And to relieve some of the stress you're under,

Let's go see the Fortune Fairy of Innocence and Wonder.

Esperanza and the Fortune Fairy of Hope
went to see the second fairy, who said:


I'm the Fortune Fairy of Innocence and Wonder.
Try to look on the bright side if you blunder.
There are so many things that you have yet to discover.
Don't let silly mistakes keep your mind under cover.
And to better deal with things that hurt you,
Let's go see the Fortune Fairy of Truth and Virtue.

They all went to see the third fairy,
who said:


I'm the Fortune Fairy of Truth and Virtue.
It's good to ask for help with troubles you get into.
Always tell the truth to a trusted friend
or grown-up like your mom or dad
So they can help you if things get really bad.
For now, let's try to put your problems behind us
By visiting the Fortune Fairy of Generosity and Kindness.

When they found the fourth fairy, she said:

I'm the Fortune Fairy of Generosity and Kindness.
Know that to be selfish is a form of blindness.
Give of yourself and always be respectful.
Be considerate and never be neglectful.
Try not to get easily discouraged.
Be like the Fortune Fairy of Strength and Courage.

So, they went to find the fifth fairy,
who said:


I'm the Fortune Fairy of Strength and Courage, my dear
Be strong, be brave and do not fear.
Learn from whatever gives you tears.
Let it build your character so you can be fierce.
Then, fight for truth, justice and integrity
With the help of the Fortune Fairy of Respect and Dignity.

The group went to see the sixth fairy,

who said:


I'm the Fortune Fairy of Respect and Dignity.

Value yourself: mind, body and spirituality.

Don't give others the power to put you down.

Always hold your head high as if wearing a crown.

Hear others out but also listen to your conscience.

For more on that, let's see the Fortune Fairy of Confidence.

The seventh fairy said:


I'm the Fortune Fairy of Confidence
Here to help you build resilience.
Always love yourself but don't be selfish,
And be proud of everything that you accomplish.
Believe in yourself with pride and determination.
And now let's listen to the Fortune Fairy of Imagination.

They then visited the eighth fairy, who said:


I'm the Fortune Fairy of Imagination,
Including resourcefulness, creativity and invention.
Some people say, "Think outside the box."
But I have to add, "Think smart like a fox."
Don't let yourself get blocked with a lot of craziness.
Instead, let's listen to the
Fortune Fairy of Happiness.

When they found the ninth fairy,
she said:


I'm the Fortune Fairy of Happiness,
Full of laughter, joy and cheerfulness.
Make your own happiness and enjoy life the best that you can.
Dance to your own music; always be your own biggest fan.
Think positively and try not to be moody.
Listen to the wisdom of the
Fortune Fairy of Beauty.

The tenth fairy said:


I'm the Fortune Fairy of Beauty, both inside and out.

Let me tell you what beauty is really all about.

Yes, that butterfly you chased was very attractive,

But always running after nice-looking things can be destructive.

Beauty is not what you see with your eyes but with your heart.

Now, on to the Fortune Fairy of Wisdom and Intelligence,

who's very smart.

The eleventh fairy said to
Esperanza:


I'm the Fortune Fairy of Wisdom and Intelligence,
Always making sure that everything makes sense.
Remember that you learn the most from things that are hard.
And once you've learned your lesson, you'll know to be on guard.
There'll always be ups and downs, joys and hardship,
So, let's go listen to the Fortune Fairy of Love and Friendship.

Finally, they reached the twelfth fairy, who said:


I'm the Fortune Fairy of Love and Friendship.
Remember that in any kind of relationship,
The power of love can be very strong
But never forget what's right and what's wrong.
Remember also all that the Fortune Fairies have had to say
And you will never again be lost from your way.

Then,
all the Fortune Fairies
led Esperanza to the
edge of the Fabled Fairy Forest,
where she finally saw her way.

Esperanza thanked all the Fortune Fairies by saying:

You've all been very helpful and kind
And you've given me peace of mind.
Each of you has presented me a special gift,
A piece of wisdom to remember whenever I feel adrift.
I promise to keep each one in my head and heart.
You'll always be with me even when we're apart.

With strength in her spirit,

love in her heart,

and wisdom in her mind,

Esperanza started to walk on her path,

full of hope.

For Manuela, memorialized as the Fortune Fairy of Hope,
who hoped for a better life for her children in the U.S.
Things got better as time went by.


For Angelica, represented by Esperanza,
who has been, is and forever will be my muse and raison d'être.
I never would have tapped into my
inner children's-book-author self if not for you.

# ACKNOWLEDGEMENTS

To Joaquin and the rest of my family, thanks for everything, not the least of which are your unwavering support and encouragement in all that I do. Thanks to my dear friends, each of whom has enriched my life immeasurably.

A super special shout-out to Tom McCafferty, author of the trilogy *The Wise Ass, An Alien Appeal,* and *Kissing My Ass Goodbye,* whose support got me started on this incredible "Second Act" journey. To all my early readers, thanks from the bottom of my heart for taking the time to read Hope and Fortune and for giving me invaluable feedback.

To Santiago Cornejo and the other artists at Enroc Illustrations: Thank you for your immense talent and great patience with my seemingly never-ending edits and detailed instructions.

Thanks to Princeton University, for giving me permission to use the school's shield logo in the rendering of the Fortune Fairy of Wisdom and Intelligence.

Finally, to Reagan Rothe and the entire team at Black Rose Writing – I cannot thank you enough for taking a chance on me.

# ABOUT THE AUTHOR

A first-generation immigrant to the U.S. from the Philippines, Marissa Bañez is a graduate of Princeton University and a lawyer licensed to practice in New York, California and New Jersey. She has published legal articles for the prestigious New York Law Journal and the American Bar Association, but her true passion in writing is in her children's stories. She currently lives in New York City with her husband and daughter, whose childhood was filled with many original stories and puppet shows made up entirely by her mom. In her free time, Marissa likes to travel, design and sew clothes, cook, binge-watch *Star Trek* shows and Korean dramas, and occasionally strum a guitar.

# BLACK ROSE writing™

© 2023 by Marissa Bañez
Ilustrations © 2023 by Marissa Bañez

All rights reserved. No part of this book may be reproduced, stored in a retrieval system or transmitted in any form or by any means without the prior written permission of the publishers, except by a reviewer who may quote brief passages in a review to be printed in a newspaper, magazine or journal.

The final approval for this literary material is granted by the author.

First printing

This is a work of fiction. Names, characters, businesses, places, events and incidents are either the products of the author's imagination or used in a fictitious manner. Any resemblance to actual persons, living or dead, or actual events is purely coincidental.

ISBN: 978-1-68513-117-3
PUBLISHED BY BLACK ROSE WRITING
www.blackrosewriting.com

Printed in the United States of America

Princeton University's permission to use the Princeton University Shield logo in this book does not imply any endorsement of any product or service by the university in connection with this book.  Princeton retains its exclusive right, title and interest in and to the Shield logo.  The author's use of the Shield logo in no way represents any claim of ownership or any interest in the Shield logo beyond the limited permission of use granted by the University

CPSIA information can be obtained
at www.ICGtesting.com
Printed in the USA
BVHW020537201022
649223BV00001B/2

9 781685 131173